Fu
Grandma

Om
KIDZ
An imprint of **Om** Books International

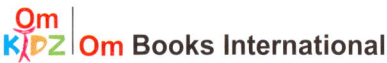

Om KIDZ | Om Books International

Reprinted in 2021

Corporate & Editorial Office
A-12, Sector 64, Noida 201 301
Uttar Pradesh, India
Phone: +91 120 477 4100
Email: editorial@ombooks.com
Website: www.ombooksinternational.com

Sales Office
107, Ansari Road, Darya Ganj
New Delhi 110 002, India
Phone: +91 11 4000 9000
Email: sales@ombooks.com
Website: www.ombooks.com

© Om Books International 2017

ISBN: 978-93-86108-86-9

Printed in India

10 9 8 7 6 5 4 3 2

Hi Nadia enjoy reading this book
with Grandma Ammamma. With loads of
Love, kisses and blessings from

Fun with Dadiamma.

Grandma

Paste your
photograph here

My name is

_____

It **was the** summer holidays.
Ben was full of **joy**. He **was**
going to visit **his** grandma.
She lived on a farm.

Ben's **mom** drove **him** to Grandma's house in their **car**. Grandma's house **was** on a hill. It **was** next to a **big** tree.

"Grandma!" said **Ben** when he **saw her**. He **ran** to **her and** gave **her** a **big hug**.

"It is so good to **see you, Ben**," said Grandma.

"**Ben**," said **Mom**, "Don't trouble your Grandma. I will be back in a **few** hours. **You** will be a good **boy**, won't **you**?"

Mum kissed **Ben and** drove away in **the car**. Grandma **and Ben** said **bye** to **her**.

"What do we do **now**?" **Ben** asked **his** Grandma.

Grandma smiled. "**Let** us go **say** hello to **the** animals," **she** said.

Ben was excited. He **had** never seen farm animals.

Grandma **and Ben** walked **out** of **the** farmhouse. They walked down **the** garden path into **the** farm.

There **was** an **old** fence behind Grandma's house. There were many birds **and** animals in it. **Ben** felt afraid. He **hid** behind **his** Grandma.

"Don't be afraid," said Grandma.
She took **Ben** to a **sty**. "**Ben**, this
is a **sty**," **she** said, "Penny **the pig**
lives here."

"Oink! Oink!" said Penny **the pig**.

Ben laughed. "Oink! Oink!" said **Ben and fed her hay**.

Then, Grandma took **Ben** to **the** coop.

"**Let** us **see** if Haley **the hen has** laid an **egg**," **she** said.

Grandma picked up Haley **the hen**. There **was** an **egg** under **her**.

Ben picked up **the egg**. He **put** it in **his** pocket.

He petted Haley **the hen**. "Cluck! Cluck!" **she** said.

Ben's grandma took **him** to meet
Harry **the** horse **and Cal the cow**.
They greeted **him** with a neigh
and a **moo**.

Soon, it **was** time **for Ben** to go home.

He kissed **his** Grandma goodbye.

"Visit again soon," said Grandma.

"I will," promised **Ben**.

What a **fun day** it **had** been at Grandma's farm!

What did Grandma and Ben find under the hen? Trace the dots to find out.

Circle the three-letter words shown on the leaves below.

hay

hug

hid

egg

farm

on

pig

hen

tree

bye

Circle the odd word out.

 **1**   Pig   Cow   Hen

 **2**   Red   Blue   Box

 **3**   Egg   Mum   Ben

 **4**   Oink   Moo   Big

Know your words

Sight Words

was	you	old	out
the	few	him	for
joy	bye	moo	has
his	now	fun	
she	let	her	
big	had	and	

Naming Words

Ben	boy	hay	Cal
Mom	sty	hen	cow
car	pig	egg	day

Doing Words

saw	hid	ran	see
hug	fed	say	put